Traitor's Gate

by

Catherine MacPhail

Illustrated by Karen Donnelly

For my son, David,
who just loves history!

First published in 2005 in Great Britain by
Barrington Stoke Ltd, Sandeman House, Trunk's Close,
55 High Street, Edinburgh EH1 1SR
www.barringtonstoke.co.uk

ISBN 1-842992-91-0

Printed in Great Britain by Bell & Bain Ltd

Barrington Stoke gratefully acknowledges support from the
Scottish Arts Council towards the publication of the
fyi series

Contents

Chapter 1
School Trip

"I need the loo!" Lizzie said.

"Trust you! You should have gone before we came." Her brother, Spider, was fed up. Not just with Lizzie. He was always fed up with Lizzie. But with being here, at Edinburgh Castle, on this boring school trip.

"And there is Traitor's Gate." The tour guide (he'd asked them to call him Robby) pointed up to a gate with an iron grill over it, built into the steep rock walls. "Traitors were thrown to their death from there."

"I wonder if tour guides were ever thrown over?" Spider said.

Mr Fisher, their teacher, turned to the class. "Isn't this interesting, children?"

"I've had more fun watching paint dry," Spider said.

Mr Fisher glared at him. "You'll be writing an essay on Robert the Bruce when we get back to school. So you'd better listen."

It wasn't that Spider didn't like history. But it was better when you saw it in a film, like *Braveheart*. He loved all the gory bits, but walking round Edinburgh Castle in the rain just wasn't the same. *I mean*, Spider thought, *you've got to bring history to life to make it interesting for children!*

Of course he knew about Robert the Bruce. That's where his nickname came from. Spider. Because like Bruce's Spider, he never gave up. Spider had tried six times to get into the football team and they wouldn't let him in. They said he was rubbish. But Spider had practised and practised and at last, on his seventh try, they had let him play. He told this story to Robby.

“Ah yes, Bruce’s spider.” Robby closed his eyes. “Hiding in a cave, Bruce watched the spider spin its web. Six times Bruce had been defeated and six times he watched the spider try to swing from one end of the cave to the other to finish its web. On the seventh try it got there, and Bruce took that as a signal that he too would win on the seventh try.”

Spider grinned.

"A great story," Robby said. "But not a bit of truth in it. It's just a story."

From then on Spider decided that Robby knew nothing. The spider story was his favourite one about Bruce.

Lizzie tugged at his sleeve. "I need the loo," she said again.

"Shut up about the loo."

Robby was watching Spider, waiting for him to shut up. Spider tried to put on his interested face. Lizzie said it made him look as if he needed the toilet too.

"And so, here is the setting for Robert the Bruce's final struggle. Robert the Bruce had been fighting for control of Scotland since 1311."

Spider checked his watch. "And it's now 14:02 and I've not had my lunch." Spider laughed. No-one else did.

Robby took no notice of him and carried on. "Now the year is 1314. A huge English army is on its way to Scotland, led by Edward II. Robert the Bruce and his men have taken almost every castle in Scotland, one by one. They have used surprise tactics to capture these castles. Under cover of darkness, they swam the moats, they climbed the walls. They used cunning. Have you heard of the Trojan Horse?"

Spider called out, "My old man backed it on Saturday. It came in last." He laughed. No-one else did.

Mr Fisher glared at him. "I'm getting very fed up with you, Spider."

Robby went on, "The Greeks hid inside a wooden horse. The Trojans dragged it inside the city walls. During the night the Greeks crept out and captured the city. That is the way the Scots took Linlithgow Castle in 1313, hiding in a hay wagon. They used it just like a Trojan Horse. Can you imagine it?"

Spider tried, but all he could imagine was Mel Gibson in *Braveheart* with blue paint on his face.

"Edinburgh Castle was the greatest prize. Here, Sir Thomas Randolph massed his troops. Here, they would fight the English and take back the castle."

Even Spider was getting interested. "There was no way to get into the castle. Then an informer told them about a secret path." He pointed up the craggy rocks that rose to the castle walls. "Up there, on the north face of the crag."

"My sister could climb up there," Spider said proudly. "Lizzie can climb anywhere."

Lizzie beamed. But she could. She was always in trouble for climbing.

Robby went on, "While some of the troops attacked the East Gate of the castle, Randolph and 30 of his men climbed the north crag. They used rope ladders to get over the walls. They opened the gates. Edinburgh Castle was theirs!"

A loud cheer went up from the class.

It was clear Robby loved telling this story. "Bruce went on to win the Battle of Bannockburn in the same year. The greatest victory in Scottish history."

Spider pretended to swing an axe above his head. "I wish I'd lived then. I wish, I wish, I wish."

Mr Fisher said, "Be careful, Spider. They say when you wish for something five times, you get your wish."

Five times, Spider thought, and to himself he said again for the fifth time, "I wish."

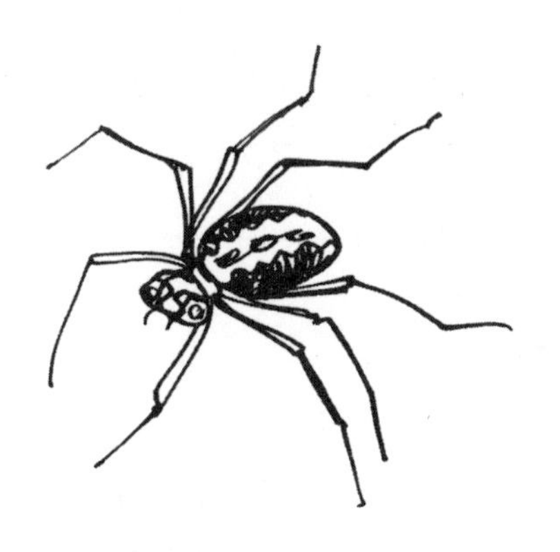

Chapter 2
I wish ...

Inside the castle Spider asked Robby if he could take one of the axes from the wall.

"You'll only chop someone's head off with it," Mr Fisher said.

"He couldn't even lift it," Robby said.

"I'm stronger than I look," Spider told him.

He asked if he could fire the one o'clock gun.

"You'll only blow up Edinburgh," Mr Fisher said.

And all the time Lizzie kept banging on about the loo.

In the end, Spider gave in.

"OK, there's the loo." He pointed to a sign leading down a narrow passage. "I'll wait for you."

"Better tell Mr Fisher where we're going," Lizzie said.

"He'll only tell us there's a really interesting brick we should be looking at."

Lizzie hesitated. "I'm not going down there by myself, Spider. Mum said you weren't to let me out of your sight."

What choice did he have? His mum would kill him if he didn't look after his sister.

They walked down the dark passage, turned a corner and found themselves facing a brick wall.

"Where are the loos?" Lizzie asked. But there were no more signs. It was dark here, and the walls were damp and cold.

"We must have taken a wrong turning," Spider said.

A chill wind blew all around them.

Spider wanted to get back to the group. He didn't like it here. He looked behind him, hoping to see a few others from his class, but there was only a mist blowing over the cobbles and a funny kind of quiet.

"Let's go back," he said. "This place is giving me the creeps."

As they walked back up the alley they began to hear noises again. People running, men shouting. Spider was glad about that. Because for a moment, just a moment, he'd had a strange feeling that everything was different.

He pulled at his sister's sleeve. "Come on, Lizzie, let's find the class."

And that's when it happened. Something whizzed past his face. It was only when it crashed into the door behind him that Spider saw what it was.

An axe.

He yelled out angrily, "Hey, that was really dangerous. Who did that?"

A great hairy hand grabbed him by the neck and lifted him off the ground. A voice roared at him.

"And what are you doing here?"

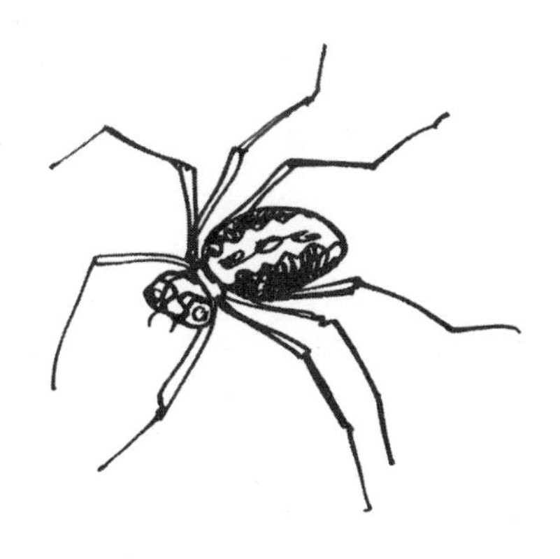

Chapter 3
Out of Time

Spider was held dangling in the air. Lizzie was screaming. The sounds of cries and yells were all around them. Men were running everywhere, all oddly dressed. Although he was scared, Spider's brain was working the whole thing out. They had been caught in the middle of a mock battle.

He'd heard of things like this. A bunch of daft men, dressed up in clothes from olden times, running around waving plastic spears, and pretending to act out old battles.

Spider struggled to be free. “Let me go!” he yelled.

The face he stared up into was the scariest he’d ever seen. A face full of scars, covered with wild hair, with a stubble of a beard and rotting teeth. He also had the worst case of BO that Spider had ever come across. Had he never heard of deodorant?

"What are you doing here?" the man growled.

Spider tried again to shake himself free. "I'm here with my class. That's my sister." He tried not to sound scared. "And I'll get my dad on you for shaking me like this."

The man suddenly dropped Spider to the ground. "You're a Scot," he said.

Spider jumped to his feet. "And proud of it!" He brushed himself down and looked around. "And by the way, I think it's dangerous to use real axes. You could have chopped my head off."

It was then Spider noticed a man being carried past them. He had an arrow sticking out of his shoulder. Blood dripped on the ground. "Nice touch," he said, "but not very real looking."

Lizzie followed his gaze. She screamed. “Spider, it looks real to me.”

“That’s because you’ve not seen the horror films I’ve seen, Lizzie.”

The big man grabbed him again, this time by the hair. “Who sent you here?”

Spider yelled, “Right! That was the last straw, mister. You’re in trouble. What’s your name?”

“No, you’re in trouble.”

Spider looked round his men. *A scruffy-looking bunch*, he thought. Whoever had hired those outfits should be shot. The man picked out the youngest, a boy who looked hardly older than Spider himself.

“Thomas,” he said, “guard them well. We’ll be back later.”

The boy, Thomas, saluted. “Yes, Constable.”

Was this man a policeman? Spider would be complaining about him later.

Spider grabbed the man's arm. "Hey, never mind coming back later. Just let us go now."

The Constable bent over Spider. Spider shrank back. This man's bad breath was nearly as bad as his BO. "We're never going to let you go," the Constable told him. "You are going to be thrown from Traitor's Gate, as spies."

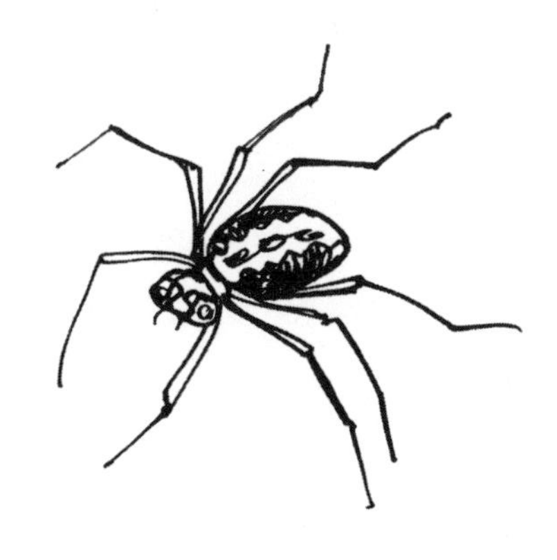

Chapter 4

Battle Stations!

Spider shouted after the man as they hurried away. “Hey, this is carrying a joke too far!” He looked round at Thomas. “What does he mean, spies?”

Thomas gave him a push. “There are spies everywhere. Only yesterday the commander of our castle, Sir Piers, was thrown into the dungeon. He’s an old friend of Robert the Bruce. The Constable has taken over his command. We can trust no-one."

He was talking as if this was real. "Come on. Game over. What school are you from?" Spider asked.

Thomas, his face streaked with dirt, stared at him. "School? I am a soldier. And this is not a game."

As if on cue, a flaming arrow flew over the castle walls. There was a sudden rush of action. More soldiers appeared firing arrows over the battlements. The sky was black with arrows.

Real arrows.

But that couldn't be, Spider thought. He was beginning to get a really bad feeling about this.

Lizzie grabbed her brother's arm. "This isn't a mock battle, Spider. This is real."

"Of course it is," Thomas said. "The Scots are trying to take Edinburgh Castle. But they will not win. We will fight to the death for the king."

Spider wasn't going to listen to that. "The king being Robert the Bruce, by the way," he said.

Thomas glared at him. "King Edward II is our king."

"King Edward – I remember Robby telling us about him. He was the Hammer of the Scots," Lizzie said.

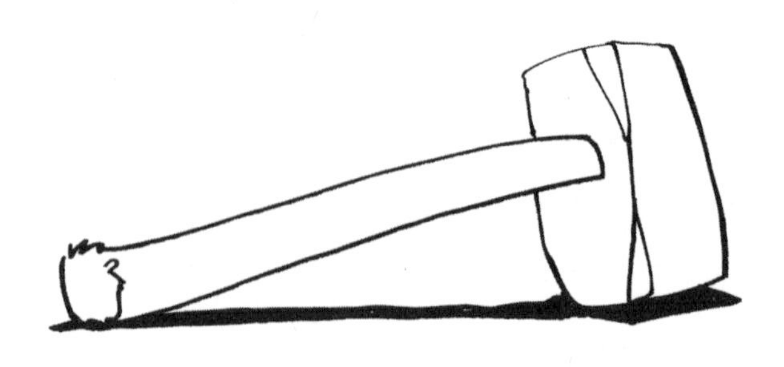

Thomas shook his head. “No, that was his father. Edward I, a great warrior, my father said. A brave soldier.”

“Was that the one they called Longshanks?” Now Spider remembered too. “Did that mean he had long legs?”

Thomas went on. “Yes, Longshanks. But this king, Edward II, is his son.” Thomas looked all around to make sure no-one could hear him. "I should not say this, but my father says he is weak and useless."

"Not like Robert the Bruce," said Spider.

Thomas spat on the ground. "He is a bandit. The ruler of a gang of criminals. King Edward is even now on his way north, with a great army. We will defeat him easily."

"That's what you think. But we know what's going to happen, don't we, Lizzie?"

Lizzie agreed. "Yes, we do. You're going to lose."

Thomas' face went white. "But we English have the greatest army in the world. The greatest archers." He said it proudly.

Spider grinned. "Maybe, but we are going to kick your butt at the Battle of Bannockburn."

"How do you know all this?" Thomas asked.

Another voice angrily repeated his words. The Constable's voice. "Yes, how exactly *do* you know all this?"

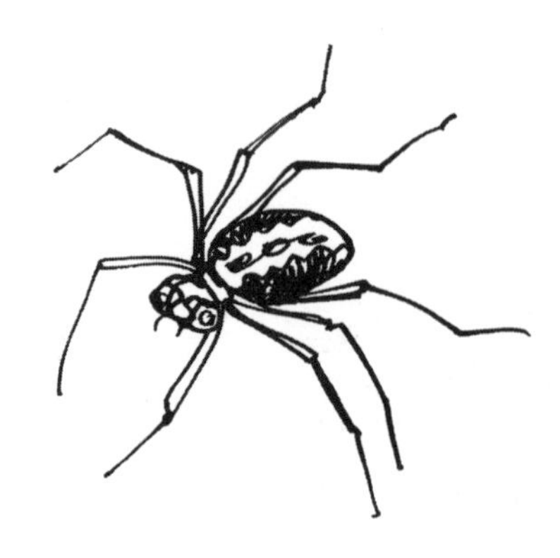

Chapter 5

On the Run!

The Constable reached out to grab Spider. Spider tried to dart past him, but his way was blocked by four huge English spearmen. *This can't be happening*, Spider thought. *Any moment now Mr Fisher will come round the corner with the rest of the class. He'll yell at me, and give me a hundred lines.* How he longed for a hundred lines.

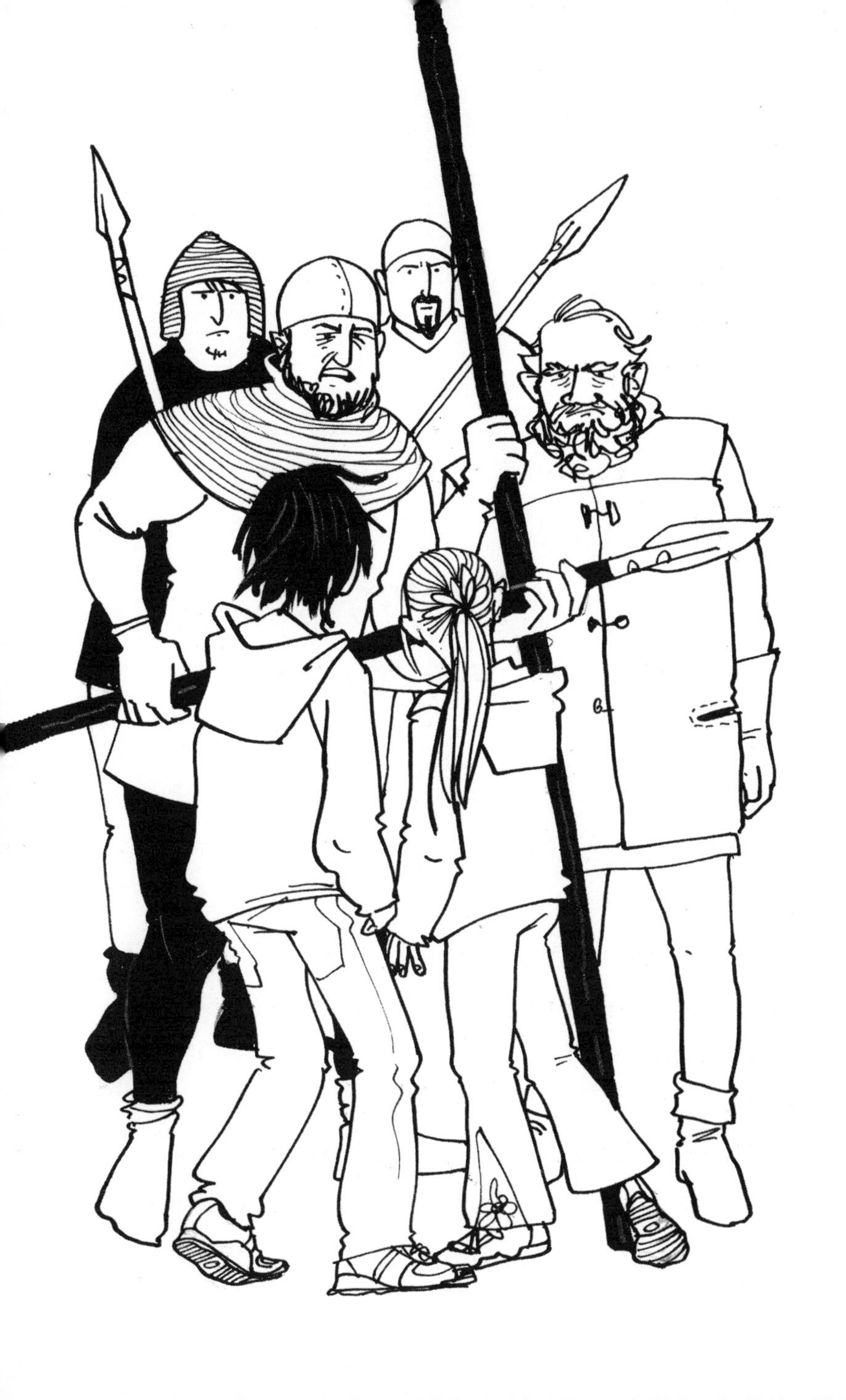

Spider was afraid. He could tell by his sister's face that she was afraid too.

The Constable shook Spider as if he was a rag doll. "Tell me how you know these things!" he demanded.

Lizzie shouted, "Because we're not from here, we're from ..."

Spider yelled to stop Lizzie saying another word. He just knew that if she told them they were from the future they would be in even more trouble.

"We're from Glasgow," he said.

The Constable looked stern. "You said we would be defeated at the Battle of Bannockburn."

Spider kept thinking about the man with the arrow in his shoulder, the blood dripping on the ground. Real blood. He knew that now. He thought he was going to throw up.

"Just a wild guess," he said.

The Constable lifted his spear and held it against Spider's throat. "Tell me everything you know, boy."

What could Spider say? What would they do? For a long moment, he just looked into

the Constable's eyes. He heard the sounds of battle all around.

At that very moment, his mobile phone began to ring.

Spider gasped. The Constable let him go and stepped back as if he had been stung. Even Thomas drew back. There was fear in all their faces. Spider pulled the phone from his pocket. It was Mr Fisher's number. Spider yelled into the phone, "Come and get us. Quick! We're in trouble."

But all he could hear in reply was static, a crackle, and then nothing.

Spider looked around. All the men looked afraid. He took a chance and held his mobile high in the air. "See. I have great power. Let us go."

It didn't work. The Constable roared. "They know the future. They have magic powers. Grab them. They will be flung from Traitor's Gate, as witches."

Chapter 6

Get me out of here!

"Not on your nellie!" Spider yelled. "Run, Lizzie!"

They darted between the soldiers who were taken by surprise. But more than that the soldiers were scared. Spider held out his mobile phone as if it was a magic wand, and the men fell back, terror in their eyes.

It gave them, just, the moments they needed to get away. A second later the Constable was shouting, ordering his men to catch them.

"Where are we going, Spider?" Lizzie could hardly speak.

"We're getting out of this castle," he said.

They could hear shouts and yells as more soldiers joined in the chase. Spider pulled his sister into a doorway to get their breath back.

"How could this happen? How did we go back in time?" Lizzie asked.

Spider didn't know the answer to that. But they were here now and they had to escape. Spider had never been so scared. Here was real life danger. He couldn't switch it off like one of his DVDs or his computer games. People had once lived with this fear, at a time when fighting was normal, when boys his age were expected to go into battle and kill. He thought again of that dripping blood and felt sick.

"Spider, they're coming closer."

And they were. If Spider didn't think of something soon they were going to be caught.

"There has to be a way out of here," he said, almost to himself.

Lizzie gasped. "There *is* a way," she said.

At that very moment a figure loomed in front of them, his spear held ready to strike.

Spider almost screamed. Then he saw it was Thomas.

Thomas wasn't smiling. "Come with me."

Lizzie said softly, "They're going to kill us, Thomas. They're going to throw us from Traitor's Gate."

"You're spies. You're witches. You deserve to die," Thomas said, but didn't sound as if he believed it. "If I am the one to catch you, I might be sent home as a reward."

"What if you get made an officer instead?" Lizzie said. "You might be sent into even more battles."

Spider could tell Thomas didn't know what to do. "I don't want to be a soldier. I want to go home, to my family."

Lizzie saw their chance. "Then let us go home too, Thomas. We're not spies. Honest. Pretend you never saw us."

"Someone else will only catch you," Thomas said. "There is no way out of this castle, unless you are flung from Traitor's Gate."

"We'll take our chances," Lizzie told him.

Thomas backed away. *If he'd been born in my time*, thought Spider, *all he would be worried about was whether he'd be picked for the school football team.*

Thomas took one last look at them. He smiled. "Good luck," he said, and then he was gone.

Spider turned to his sister. "Right, clever clogs. So how do we get out of here?"

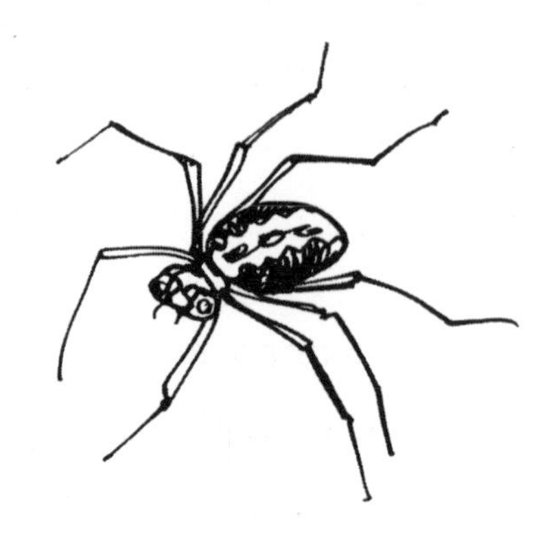

Chapter 7

Good old Lizzie

Lizzie's voice was a whisper. "You remember what Robby told us, about the secret path?"

Robby, Spider thought, *the boring tour guide.* How he would love to see him again.

Lizzie went on, "He told us about the secret path up the north crag. And if you can go up, then you must be able to go down. And I remember exactly where it was."

She dragged her brother on. They crept quickly across open spaces, hoping no-one would see them. At last they were at the castle walls.

Lizzie looked over. "It's just down there," she said.

Spider looked where she was pointing. There was a sheer wall of rock, tumbling down into darkness. He staggered back in shock. "No, Lizzie. We could never climb down that."

There were sudden shouts behind them, footsteps thundering closer. In a moment they would be found.

Spider had a sudden picture of dripping blood, his blood this time. They didn't have a choice. "Let's go," he said.

Spider's heart was beating so fast he thought it would burst. He couldn't make out anything in the blackness. Black as pitch. No brightly lit Princes Street, with its traffic and its shops. No streets at all in fact. All they could see were the dark Pentland Hills.

Above them they could hear the Constable shouting angrily. "Find them!"

They stood still and silent for a moment, until the footsteps moved off.

"Follow me," Lizzie said. Normally, Spider would never follow his sister anywhere. But his common sense told him that she was a good climber. Better than him.

Once or twice she lost her footing and sent rocks and stones hurtling below. Then they would both stop, pressed against the rock, holding their breath. They listened for the sounds of soldiers coming down after them.

Down and down they went, clinging onto rock, slipping on the wet stones.

“Almost there,” Lizzie said.

They were going to make it, Spider thought. And then what? What were they going to do after that? How would they ever get back?

They had just made it to the bottom when a gruff voice bellowed, “Who goes there?”

Not again! Spider thought.

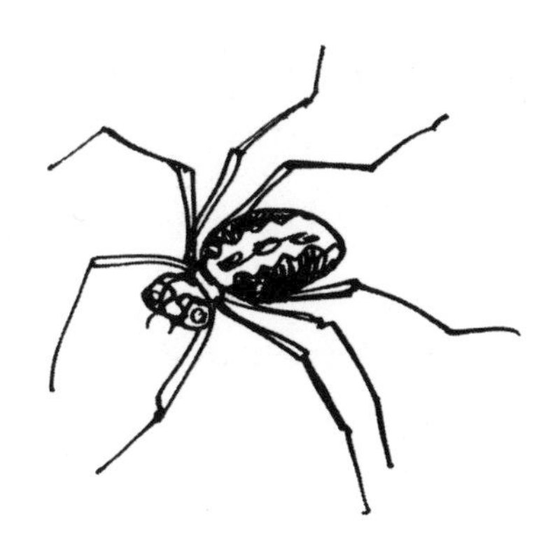

Chapter 8

Back to the Future

"Where have you come from?"

Spider couldn't see the soldier's face. He could only see his dark eyes through the eye-lets on the steel helmet he wore.

"Up there," Spider pointed up towards the castle.

“Liar!” the soldier said. “There is no way up there, and no way down. Unless they throw you over the battlements.”

They almost did, Spider wanted to tell him, but he didn’t get the chance. “Spies!” the soldier shouted. “You will die for this.”

Spider shouted back, “We’re not spies.”

Lizzie tugged at the soldier. “We’re not lying. We can show you the secret path. And if we can get down, you can get up. You can get into the castle.”

The soldier peered at them through his visor. “Show me this secret way,” he said.

Lizzie grabbed him by the arm. She climbed back up the rocks and he followed her, dragging Spider behind him. Lizzie stopped where the path seemed to open up clear to the top. She told the soldier almost step by step how to get up to the castle walls. Spider was well impressed.

“Come with me. You must see Sir Thomas Randolph. Tell him what you have told me.”

Lizzie shook her head. Spider just shook. “No. You tell Sir Thomas that you know the way into the castle. Please, we just want to go home.”

Spider joined in. “Yes, you be the hero. Show the army the secret way up to the castle and you’ll be remembered forever.”

The soldier's eyes glinted. "Me? William Francis?"

"Yes, you. Tell them you know the secret path, only you," Spider said.

He could almost read the soldier's mind. He would become a hero, his story told in the history books. It took William Francis only a second to make up his mind. "I shall let you go. See the mercy of the men of Robert the Bruce."

"Come on, Lizzie, we're getting out of here!" Spider began running. Any moment now a battle was about to start and he didn't want to be in the middle of it.

"I thought you liked fighting and blood and all that," Lizzie said.

He pulled his sister on. "In films, on TV, yes. In real life I've decided I prefer peace and quiet." He thought about that. "Most of all the peace bit."

They kept on running, not knowing where they were going. "How are we going to get back, Spider?" Lizzie was almost crying.

He tried to think what he did to get here in the first place. It was then he remembered Mr Fisher's words. "Say it aloud five times and you may just get your wish."

It was worth a try. "I wish. I wish. I wish. I wish ... I wish."

Spider opened his eyes. Nothing seemed to have changed.

Lizzie was shivering. "We're going to be stuck here forever."

"I wish. I wish, I wish, I wish, I wish!" Spider yelled again.

And suddenly, Mr Fisher's face zoomed down at them. "Where have you two been? We've been looking all over for you!"

It had worked! Spider began to babble. "We were transported back in time, sir. The

English were going to kill us. They thought we were spies."

Lizzie jumped in. "Then they thought we were witches. That was when the mobile phone went off."

"And you switched me off, boy!" the teacher roared.

Spider ignored that. "And we had to escape. They were going to throw us down from Traitor's Gate."

"So we came down the secret path. The one Robby told us about."

Mr Fisher shook his head. "I've never heard such rubbish in all my life!" he said.

"It's the truth, sir."

But Mr Fisher wasn't listening. "You are in real trouble this time, boy," he said.

Spider was so grateful to be back he thanked him.

"Maybe we just imagined it all, Lizzie. Could it really have happened?" Spider said as they hurried after the teacher.

Robby fell in beside them. “You just got carried away with the wonderful story. I am so glad that you were listening.”

“Robby, what was the name of the informer who told them about the secret path?” Lizzie asked.

“Ah, it made that soldier’s name and his fortune,” Robby said. “He was rewarded by Robert the Bruce and became rich and famous. His name was William Francis.”

Lizzie gasped and grabbed her brother’s hand. That was one part of the story they had never heard. There was no way they could have known that.

Spider was trying to take it all in. Had it really happened? Already it seemed like a dream. All he was sure of now was that it was better to read about history than to live it.

"I've just remembered something, Spider," Lizzie said.

"What?" Spider looked at her and she giggled.

"I still need the loo."

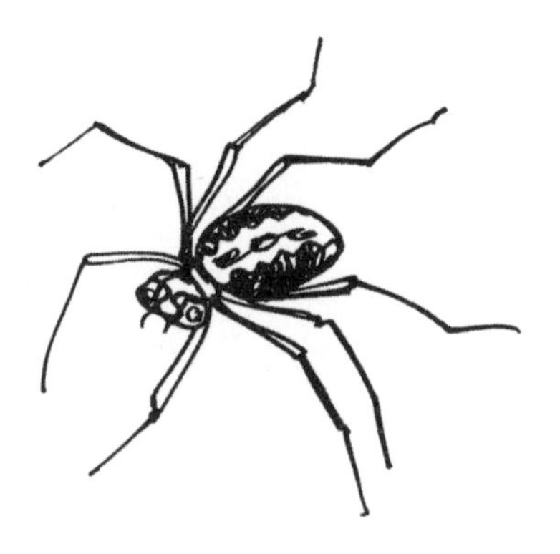

Spider's notebook

Dead spider, circa 1420 (or twenty past two to you morons)

~~Fassinating~~ ~~Fastenat~~ Interesting facts about Robert the Bruce

1. He was born on July 11th, 1274. He was crowned King at Scone in 1306.

2. It was very unlucky to be a brother of Robert the Bruce. They all died horribly. Hung, drawn and quartered. This means they were hung till they were nearly dead, then their insides were pulled out, and then what was left of their bodies was cut into four bits.

This is not the kind of thing we need to know, spider!

I think it's interesting, sir.

3. Robert the Bruce died on June 7th, 1329. His dying wish was that his heart be taken on the Crusades. So his friend, the Black Douglas, carried Bruce's heart with him into battle at Tebas de Ardales. The Black Douglas died in this battle, but Bruce's heart was carried back to Scotland and is buried at Melrose Abbey. The rest of him is buried in Dunfermline. I think it was time he was joined up again. He is a national hero, after all.

How often do I have to tell you, Spider? Keep to the facts!

Sorry, sir.

The events that led to the Battle of Bannockburn

1. 1286 – King Alexander III of Scotland falls off his horse, then falls off a cliff, then cracks his skull, and drowns. (Talk about unlucky!)

2. His only heir, the Maid of Norway, is shipwrecked on the way to Scotland and then falls ill and dies of disease.

(Bad luck must run in that family.)

3. The nobles of Scotland ask King Edward I of England, Longshanks himself, to help decide who should be the king of Scotland.

(They must have been off their rockers!)

Spider! How often have I got to tell you? Just give us the facts.

4. King Edward chooses John Baliol on condition that John Baliol promises that Edward will be the real big boss of the country.

(And he agreed! Was he off his rocker as well?)

5. A year later John Baliol changes his mind. Nobody is going to be his boss.

So Edward invades Scotland, captures Baliol and makes a real fool of him in front of his whole army. (What a red face!)

6. After that, Baliol is nicknamed Toom Tabard. That means "empty coat"

(Not much of a nickname if you ask me anything. We could have come up with a better one in my school.)

But after that, King Edward helps himself to Scotland. And the fight for freedom begins. First with William Wallace (What a hero!) and then with Robert the Bruce. And at Bannockburn, Scottish freedom was won.

Interesting facts about the Battle of Bannockburn

1. It lasted two days.
(Not if I had been there.)

2. The English far outnumbered the Scots. Talk about David and Goliath! Edward II had 2,500 heavy cavalry.

(That means they were on horses, sir.)

Thank you, Spider. I would never have known that myself.

3. There were 2,000 archers. (That means they had bows and arrows.)

4. And 500 light cavalry.

(Does that mean they were all skinny?)

5. And a well-trained infantry.

(Infantry, sir. Does that mean they were just children?)

No, Spider. It means they were on foot. Now, shut up and get on with your notes!

6. But Robert the Bruce had a brilliant plan. He was going to trap the army on a path between the woods around Bannockburn village. And he was going to attack them there.

That's called an ambush.

Spider, what have I told you?

Sorry, sir.

7. Robert the Bruce was almost killed before the battle even began. An English knight called Henry de Bohun saw Bruce on his horse and charged at him. He nearly got him too. But Bruce was too quick for him, and it was Henry de Bohun who was killed instead.

But if he had killed King Robert, history would have been different, eh?

8. By the way, the Scots won the Battle of Bannockburn.

After the Battle of Bannockburn

1. After the Battle of Bannockburn the nobles of Scotland got together with Robert the Bruce and signed the Declaration of Arbroath on April 6th, 1320, the most famous document in Scottish history. The American Declaration of Independence was based on it and the United States of America has declared April 6th Tartan Day.

Good work, Spider! I didn't know that!

Thank you, sir. I read it in a book.

2. Here is an extract from the Declaration of Arbroath:

"It is in truth not for glory, nor riches, nor honours that we are fighting, but for freedom – for that alone, which no honest man gives up but with life itself."

Yes!!!! Freedom, my favourite word, sir.

Mine too, Spider.

What else was happening in 1314?

1. A grandson of Ghengis Khan, the great Mongol leader, was terrorising Europe with his army, invading all sorts of places. His army was called the Golden Horde.

(What a brilliant name, sir. You can just imagine them, pouring over the horizon, their helmets and their shields shining like gold in the sun.)

why can't you write like this when I ask you to write an essay, Spider?

Because history's really interesting, sir.

2. The Mameluke family ruled Egypt and they used to be slaves. Imagine, slaves becoming the rulers of Egypt. Their main man, Al Malik an Nasir, signed a peace treaty with the Mongols that brought many years of peace and prosperity.

(It's nice to know that some good things were happening.)

3. Lewis of Bavaria was the ruler of the Holy Roman Empire.

(Lewis, he sounds Scottish, sir.)

(Some people spell it Louis, Spider.)

Well, whatever, he ruled along with Frederick the Fair.

(I don't know if that meant he was blond or just a decent kind of king, sir.)

4. And in Japan, the Hojo family were the rulers.

I am most impressed, Spider.

Other interesting facts

1. Just like the Scots with the Declaration of Arbroath, the English also have a great historic document they can be proud of. It is called the Magna Carta, (that means the Great Charter) and it is like the Bill of Rights. It was signed by King John at Runnymede in 1215.

(See, people were learning all the time, sir, that everybody has got to have rights.)

A very wise comment, spider.

2. Just like Robert the Bruce, another famous person who isn't joined up is Oliver Cromwell. His head is buried in Cambridge, but his body is on the site of Tyburn Gallows in London.

(Before you say anything, sir, I think that's interesting.)

3. America hadn't been invented yet.

America was not invented, Spider. It was discovered, by Christopher Columbus in 1492. He travelled across the Atlantic with his fleet of three ships, the Pinta, the Nina and the Santa Maria.

Well, if they hadn't discovered it I think it would have had to have been invented.

4. There is also some evidence that a Scotsman called Henry Sinclair, the Earl of Orkney, discovered America

a long time before Columbus.

(Honest, sir, I read it in a book.)

5. If you needed the loo in 1314, you probably used a hole in the ground. If you were poor you had very little choice.

I think one of the best things about living now is loos that flush.

(That was Lizzie that wrote that, sir. Honest. She stole my pencil.)

what am I going to do with you two?!

6. When William the Conqueror died he was very fat and when they tried

to squeeze him into his coffin, his body exploded.

(Yuck! I wouldn't have liked to have been anywhere near that! That must have been disgusting.)

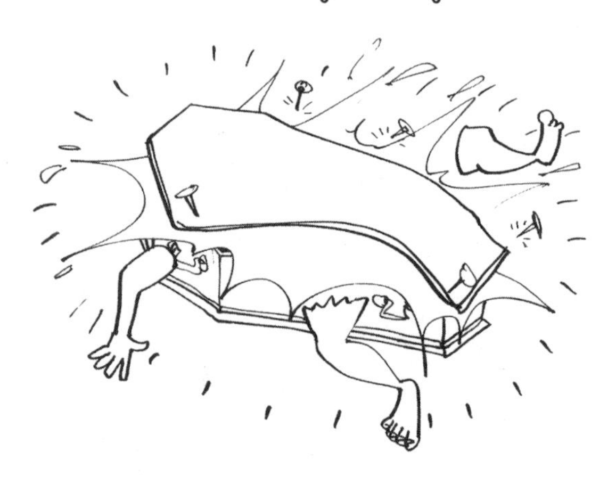

Spider! What has that got to do with Robert the Bruce?!

(It's a really interesting fact, sir. Really, really interesting. Be honest.)

Other famous people who lived in 1314

1. A famous Italian poet called Dante lived then. He wrote something called Dante's Inferno.

(Inferno means hell, sir.)

I can write poetry too, sir.

There was a young poet called Dante,
Who wanted to live with his aunty,
His mother was mad,
And so was his dad,

(I can't think of a last line, sir.)

I don't think that was the kind of poetry Dante wrote, spider.

(Pity, he might have been able to come up with a last line.)

2. The greatest traveller of the age was a Muslim called Ibn Batuta. He visited Africa, India, Asia, Europe and China.

(And he didn't even have a plane! I'd love to find out more about him, sir!)

Grisly deaths in 1314

Do we have to, Spider?

(Boys will love this, sir! I've kept the best till last!)

They were great ones for hanging, drawing and quartering. Most of all after poor old William Wallace. After the fall of Kildrummy Castle in 1306 there was a bloodbath. Edward I ordered that Neil Bruce, Robert's brother, should be drawn, hanged and beheaded.

The Earl of Atholl was hanged too. After they cut his head off they burnt his body.

Simon Fraser, another of Bruce's

supporters, was hanged and beheaded.

(That means his head was cut off with an axe, sir. They didn't do things by halves, sir, did they?)

Thank you, Spider, what would I do without you?

Anyway, after they cut off Simon Fraser's head they stuck it on a pole on London Bridge right beside the head of William Wallace.

(Imagine going home for your tea and having to pass that!)

Edward I was really cruel to the women too. Mary Bruce, Robert's sister, and Countess Isobel of Buchan were put in cages made of timber and iron and placed within the turrets of Roxburgh and Berwick Castles. They were left there for several years, before they were released.

Edward I was going to put Robert the Bruce's daughter, Marjorie, in a cage too, but luckily somebody sensible said, "Hey, wait a minute, King, she's only 12!" So he changed his mind.

I know I would not have liked to have lived then.

But it was still exciting.

The last Crusade finished in 1291 when the last stronghold fell.

People were beginning to want their rights.

And the Black Death was on its way. The most terrible disease in history. And that disease would kill millions.

Everything was changing.

And Scotland had its independence.

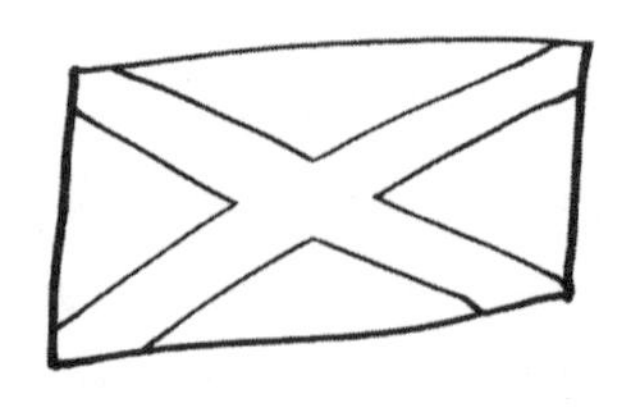

AUTHOR FACT FILE
CATHERINE MACPHAIL

If you could be anyone in history, who would you be?

If I could be anyone in history I'd pick someone preferably who didn't get their head cut off, or someone who wasn't tortured horribly, or who didn't die young from some terrible disease. That really cuts down my choices, doesn't it? But I've always loved the story of John Paul Jones, a Scotsman who founded the American navy, and then went on to found the Russian navy too. Another of my Scottish heroes is Andrew Carnegie. He emigrated to America, a poor Scottish boy, and through hard work he became one of the richest men in the country. But that's not why he's my hero. When he decided he had enough money, he gave away the rest to good causes. Because of him we have all our wonderful Carnegie libraries, and the Carnegie Medal, the greatest prize in

children's books, is named after him. What a guy!

In which period of Scottish history would it have been most fun to live?

I'd have to pick a time when loos flushed, when we had central heating and I had a vote and freedom. Come to think of it, now is the best time in Scottish history!

Who is the best King or Queen that Scotland has ever had?

I've always thought that Macbeth wasn't the villain that Shakespeare made him out to be. He was a really successful ruler and was highly thought of. In 1050 he went on a pilgrimage to Rome and is reported to have scattered money to the poor like seed. (Does that sound like a murderer?) So I've got a soft spot for the real Macbeth.

But for a second choice it would have to be James IV. Read about him! There are so many brilliant stories about him. He is considered one of the greatest kings in Scottish history and was known as the "Renaissance King". Unfortunately, he was killed at the Battle of Flodden Field, the worst defeat in Scottish history.

Are you Scottish yourself?

Yes, I am Scottish, with a touch of the Irish on my mother's side!

ILLUSTRATOR FACT FILE
KAREN DONNELLY

If you could be anyone in history, who would you be?

I'd like to try being an "ordinary person" in all different times and places in history. I think I'd always want to come home to the 21st century.

In which period of Scottish history would it have been most fun to live?

I'd like to have been a highland crofter about a thousand years ago. It probably wasn't much fun though.

Who is the best King or Queen that Scotland has ever had?

Sorry, no idea!! Can anyone suggest one for me?!

Are you Scottish yourself?

No, I'm half Irish and half English.

Barrington Stoke would like to thank all its readers for commenting on the manuscript before publication and in particular:

Daniel Agland
Padraig Baker
Joe Barrett
Samuel Bassett
Joshua Brailsford
Joshua Butt
Judy Cochand
Sean Downes
Gregor Hay
William Harris
Sarah Jane Holloway
Nicholas Jerrom
Jennifer Jones
Tom Kelleher
Lucy Kidd
Jamie Lanc
Kelly McGuinness
Mairi Marlborough
Mack Millar
Katherine Moore
Callum Peace
Lisa Rushbrook
Scott Watkins
Jonnie Willett
Mrs Williamson

Try another book in the "fyi" series! Fiction with stacks of facts

The Environment:

Connor's Eco Den by Pippa Goodhart

Football:

Stat Man by Alan Durant

The Internet:

The Doomsday Virus by Steve Barlow and Steve Skidmore

Space:

Space Ace by Eric Brown

Vikings:

The Last Viking by Terry Deary